ISAAC BASHEVIS SINGER
The Parakeet Named Dreidel

Pictures by **Suzanne Raphael Berkson**

Farrar Straus Giroux • **New York**

To Gershon —S.R.B.

Farrar Straus Giroux Books for Young Readers
175 Fifth Avenue, New York 10010

Originally published as "The Parakeet Named Dreidel" in *The Power of Light* by Isaac Bashevis Singer
Text copyright © 1980 by Isaac Bashevis Singer
Pictures copyright © 2015 by Suzanne Raphael Berkson
All rights reserved
Color separations by Bright Arts (H.K.) Ltd.
Printed in China by RR Donnelley Asia Printing Solutions Ltd.,
Dongguan City, Guangdong Province
First edition, 2015
10 9 8 7 6 5 4 3 2 1

mackids.com

Library of Congress Cataloging-in-Publication Data
Singer, Isaac Bashevis, 1904–1991.
    The parakeet named Dreidel / Isaac Bashevis Singer ; pictures by Suzanne Raphael Berkson. — First edition.
        pages cm
    "Originally published as 'The Parakeet Named Dreidel' in The Power of Light by Isaac Bashevis Singer"—
Copyright page.
    Summary: On the eighth night of Hanukkah, a family rescues a Yiddish-speaking, dreidel-playing parakeet.
    ISBN 978-0-374-30094-4 (hardback)
    ISBN 978-0-374-30096-8 (trade paperback)
    [1. Parakeets—Fiction.   2. Hanukkah—Fiction.   3. Jews—United States—Fiction.]   I. Berkson, Suzanne
Raphael, illustrator.   II. Title.

PZ7.S6167Par 2015
[E]—dc23
                                                                                        2015002960

Farrar Straus Giroux Books for Young Readers may be purchased for business or promotional use.
For information on bulk purchases please contact Macmillan Corporate and Premium Sales Department at
(800) 221-7945 x5442 or by email at specialmarkets@macmillan.com.

It happened about ten years ago in Brooklyn, New York. All day long a heavy snow was falling. Toward evening the sky cleared and a few stars appeared. A frost set in. It was the eighth day of Hanukkah, and my silver Hanukkah lamp stood on the windowsill with all candles burning. It was mirrored in the windowpane, and I imagined another lamp outside.

My wife, Esther, was frying potato pancakes.
I sat with my son, David, at a table and played
dreidel with him.

Suddenly David cried out, "Papa, look!"
And he pointed to the window.
   I looked up and saw something that
seemed unbelievable.

Outside on the windowsill stood a yellow-green bird watching the candles. In a moment I understood what had happened. A parakeet had escaped from its home somewhere, had flown out into the cold street and landed on my windowsill, perhaps attracted by the light.

A parakeet is native to a warm climate, and it cannot stand the cold and frost for very long. I immediately took steps to save the bird from freezing. First I carried away the Hanukkah lamp so that the bird would not burn itself when entering.

Then I opened the window and with a quick
wave of my hand shooed the parakeet inside.
The whole thing took only a few seconds.

In the beginning the frightened bird flew from wall to wall. It hit itself against the ceiling and for a while hung from a crystal prism on the chandelier. David tried to calm it, "Don't be afraid, little bird, we are your friends."

Presently the bird flew toward David and landed on his head,
as though it had been trained and was accustomed to people.
David began to dance and laugh with joy.

My wife, in the kitchen, heard the noise and came out to see what had happened. When she saw the bird on David's head, she asked, "Where did you get a bird all of a sudden?"

"Mama, it just came to our window."

"To the window in the middle of the winter?"

"Papa saved its life."

The bird was not afraid of us. David lifted his hand to his forehead and the
bird settled on his finger. Esther placed a saucer of millet and a dish of water on
the table, and the parakeet ate and drank. It saw the dreidel and began to push
it with its beak. David exclaimed, "Look, the bird plays dreidel."

David soon began to talk about buying a cage for the bird and also about giving it a name, but Esther and I reminded him that the bird was not ours. We would try to find the owners, who probably missed their pet and were worried about what had happened to it in the icy weather. David said, "Meanwhile, let's call it Dreidel."

That night Dreidel slept on a picture frame and woke us in the morning with its singing. The bird stood on the frame, its plumage brilliant in the purple light of the rising sun, shaking as in prayer, whistling, twittering, and talking all at the same time.

The parakeet must have belonged to a house where Yiddish was spoken, because we heard it say, *"Zeldele, geh schlofen"* (Zeldele, go to sleep), and these simple words uttered by the tiny creature filled us with wonder and delight.

The next day I posted a notice in the elevators of the neighborhood houses. It said that we had found a Yiddish-speaking parakeet.

When a few days passed and no one called, I advertised in the newspaper for which I wrote, but a week went by and no one claimed the bird. Only then did Dreidel become ours.

We bought a large cage with all the fittings and toys that a bird might want, but because Hanukkah is a festival of freedom, we resolved never to lock the cage. Dreidel was free to fly around the house whenever he pleased. (The man at the pet shop had told us that the bird was a male.)

Nine years passed and Dreidel remained with us.
We became more attached to him from day to day.

In our house Dreidel learned scores of Yiddish, English, and Hebrew words. David taught him to sing a Hanukkah song, and there was always a wooden dreidel in the cage for him to play with.

When I wrote on my Yiddish typewriter, Dreidel
would cling to the index finger of either my right or
my left hand, jumping acrobatically with every letter I
wrote. Esther often joked that Dreidel was helping me
write and that he was entitled to half my earnings.

Our son, David, grew up and entered college. One winter night he went to a Hanukkah party. He told us that he would be home late, and Esther and I went to bed early. We had just fallen asleep when the telephone rang. It was David. As a rule he is a quiet and composed young man. This time he spoke so excitedly that we could barely understand what he was saying.

It seemed that David had told the story of our parakeet to his fellow students at the party, and a girl named Zelda Rosen had exclaimed, "I am this Zeldele! We lost our parakeet nine years ago." Zelda and her parents lived not far from us, but they had never seen the notice in the newspaper or the ones posted in elevators. Zelda was now a student and a friend of David's. She had never visited us before, although our son often spoke about her to his mother.

We slept little that night. The next day Zelda and her parents came to see their long-lost pet. Zelda was a beautiful and gifted girl. David often took her to the theater and to museums. Not only did the Rosens recognize their bird, but the bird seemed to recognize his former owners.

The Rosens used to call him Tsip-Tsip, and when the parakeet heard them say "Tsip-Tsip," he became flustered and started to fly from one member of the family to the other, screeching and flapping his wings. Both Zelda and her mother cried when they saw their beloved bird alive. The father stared silently. Then he said, "We have never forgotten our Tsip-Tsip."

I was ready to return the parakeet to his original owners, but Esther and David argued that they could never part with Dreidel. It was also not necessary because that day David and Zelda decided to get married after their graduation from college. So Dreidel is still with us, always eager to learn new words and new games.

When David and Zelda marry, they will take Dreidel to their new home. Zelda has often said, "Dreidel was our matchmaker."

On Hanukkah he always gets a gift—

a mirror,

a ladder,

a swing,

a bathtub,

or a jingle bell.

He has even developed a taste for potato pancakes,
as befits a parakeet named Dreidel.